W9-BSH-469

THERE WAS AN OLD LADY WHO SWALLOWED A DRAGON!

by Lucille Colandro

Illustrated by Jared Lee

Cartwheel Books

an imprint of Scholastic Inc.

For Pam, who loves to read.
– L.C.

To Shelly Veehoff and Teresa Imperato for all that you do.
– J.L.

Text copyright © 2023 by Lucille Colandro
Illustrations copyright © 2023 by Jared D. Lee Studios

All rights reserved. Published by Scholastic Inc., *Publishers since 1920*. SCHOLASTIC, CARTWHEEL BOOKS, and associated logos are trademarks and/or registered trademarks of Scholastic Inc.

No part of this publication may be reproduced, stored in a retrieval system, or transmitted in any form or by any means, electronic, mechanical, photocopying, recording, or otherwise, without written permission of the publisher. For information regarding permission, write to Scholastic Inc., Attention: Permissions Department, 557 Broadway, New York, NY 10012.

This book is a work of fiction. Names, characters, places, and incidents are either the product of the author's imagination or are used fictitiously, and any resemblance to actual persons, living or dead, business establishments, events, or locales is entirely coincidental.

ISBN 978-1-338-87911-7

10 9 8 7 6 5 4 3 2

23 24 25 26 27

Printed in the U.S.A.   40
First edition, April 2023

There was an old lady who swallowed a dragon.
I don't know why she swallowed the dragon.
Can you imagine?

There was an old lady who swallowed a princess.
It was her wish to swallow the princess.

She swallowed the princess to guide the dragon.
I don't know why she swallowed the dragon.
Can you imagine?

There was an old lady who swallowed a knight.
It took great might to swallow the brave knight.

She swallowed the knight to soar with the princess.
She swallowed the princess to guide the dragon.

I don't know why she swallowed the dragon.
Can you imagine?

There was an old lady who swallowed a castle.
What a hassle to swallow that towering castle.

She swallowed the castle for all to assemble.
She swallowed the knight to soar with the princess.
She swallowed the princess to guide the dragon.

I don't know why she swallowed the dragon.
Can you imagine?

There was an old lady who swallowed a moat.
She didn't bloat when she swallowed the moat.

She swallowed the moat to surround the castle.

She swallowed the castle for all to assemble.
She swallowed the knight to soar with the princess.
She swallowed the princess to guide the dragon.

I don't know why she swallowed the dragon.
Can you imagine?

There was an old lady who swallowed a mermaid.
She wasn't afraid to swallow the mermaid.

She swallowed the mermaid to float in the moat.

She swallowed the moat to surround the castle.

She swallowed the castle for all to assemble.

She swallowed the knight to soar with the princess.

She swallowed the princess to guide the dragon.

I don't know why she swallowed the dragon.
Can you imagine?

There was an old lady who swallowed a book.

She really shook as she swallowed the book . . .

She closed her eyes and began to exhale...

...and out came a magical fairy tale!

Happy reading!